Sara's

Secret Journey

Sara's

Secret Journey

Patricia Lee

ISBN: 1-58930-154-4
Library of Congress Control Number: 2005904229

This book is dedicated
with love
to my family

This story is what it is because of my mother and father,
two brothers and four sisters.
Without their help I would not have been able
to create this lovely story.
Their love and strong family ties made me the person I am.

My son and daughter-in-law and daughter and
son-in-law kept telling me I should write.
My husband, Paul,
for his love and support.

Writing this book has been a wonderful experience.

Chapter

One

*I*t was a cool spring morning when thirteen-year-old Sara started walking out of the hallow in western Kentucky knowing there had to be a better life for her somewhere. With only five dollars in her small purse, she had just enough to buy a ticket for somewhere north. She was hoping to meet up with her sister and her husband. Her sister, Allie, was only fifteen years old, but she had a husband to help support her. Sara would have to lie about her age to get a job, but she knew she could do that; after all, everyone said she looked sixteen.

The next day, she arrived tired and hungry at a small bus station in Indiana, not knowing where to begin looking for her sister. But first things first—she was so hungry. It had been almost eight hours since she had eaten. As she walked down the street of the small town, it looked quite big compared to where she had come from. She spotted a sign with a big, white hat on it; it was the White Hat Diner. *This is where I will eat*, she thought. She walked in and looked around the small but nice little diner. There was a tall, red-headed man behind the counter who was wearing a white apron. At least it was supposed to be white. He was flipping burgers that smelled so good. It had been a long time since she had a meal. As she sat down, a lady with a pretty red apron said, "What are you going to have, hon?"

"I will have one of those hamburgers, please, and a cup of black coffee," she replied.

The waitress walked away to place the order. "Dan, we got a young one out there, and she looks like she is new in town."

When the waitress returned with Sara's food, Sara asked, "Could you please tell me where Court Avenue is?"

"Sure, it's the next street over."

"Thanks." Sara finished her food and started out the door. There was a sign in the window that said, "Help Wanted."

As she was looking at the sign, a voice spoke: "You need a job, little lady?"

Sara looked back over her shoulder and said, "As a matter of fact, I do!"

The tall, red-headed man said, "Come back tomorrow, and we will talk about it."

"Okay, I will." Sara said thanks as she left the diner. *Well,* she thought to herself, *I could do that job.*

She walked down the street and spotted the street sign that said Court Avenue. She reached in her purse to get the paper with the address: 916 Court Avenue. She walked a little farther, and there it was—the old, two-story house. My goodness, it was so big! She started up the stairs and saw six mailboxes, all with names on them. How would she find her sister? Then all of a sudden, she heard a voice say, "Sara, is that you?" Turning around, she saw her sister, Allie, running toward her. "What are you doing here?" Allie cried.

"I am here to get a job. Can I stay with you, please?"

"Do Mom and Dad know you left?"

"I am sure they do now. I told Mom last week I was coming to see you. She said no, that I was too young to go off by myself. But I just had to, I couldn't live there any longer."

The two sisters were so happy to see each other. They walked down the hall to a door that had a "3" on it. "Well, here is where we live," Allie announced.

Sara was so excited that Allie had her own place. It was a small apartment, only one big room with a bed in one corner and a small sink and kitchen on the other side of the room, and a sofa and a table with a lamp. It was so clean and neat, and it looked like a mansion to Sara.

"You must be tired from that bus trip," Allie said.

"Yes, I am."

"Do you want to freshen up?"

"That would be nice."

"We even have our own bathroom," Allie said. There was a small bathroom in the apartment. Sara was so thrilled because she wasn't used to an inside toilet. She went in and took a bath, and when she came out, Allie had made up the sofa for her bed. Allie said, "You can sleep here." Allie's husband worked the night shift at the local factory so he slept during the day.

"I have to get up early and go to work at the shirt factory," Allie said. She carried bundles of material up to the women who sewed. She knew how to sew, but she wasn't able to convince the man who did the hiring that she was eighteen. She was only fifteen and a half, and she wasn't as good an actress as Sara. But at least she had a job and was able to help with the expenses.

The next morning, Sara and Allie were up early. Chuck had already headed for bed. He took a minute to say hello to Sara. "We will talk later," He said to Allie. Sara was wondering if her unannounced visit might cause a problem. As her sister finished her last cup of coffee, Sara told Allie her plan to go the diner to see about a job. "Good luck, Sara. See you about six o'clock," she said.

As Sara was walking down the street, she thought, *I hope I don't have to fill out any kind of paperwork.* Her heart was pounding. She needed to convince this man at the diner that she was old enough to work and wait on tables. She knew she could do this—how hard could it be to ask people if they were ready to order?

As she walked into the diner, the red-headed man and the waitress were standing there talking. They looked up to see Sara entering the diner. "Well, hi there, little lady," the man in the cook's apron said.

"My name is Sara."

"Do you have a last name?"

"Yes, my name is Sara Stinson."

"Pleased to meet you, Sara Stinson. I am Dan, and this is my wife, Anna. We own this diner. Have you ever waited on tables before?"

"No, but I am ready to give it a shot."

They liked her attitude and her neat and clean appearance. "Show her around, Anna, and see what she thinks," the man said.

The kitchen was small, but the grill was large. "That's where most of the food is fixed," Anna explained. "It gets very busy in here, and you have to work fast."

"Anna, are you saying I got the job?" Sara asked.

"If you want, you can start right now." Anna handed her an apron. As Sara put the apron on, she thought it was strange that they didn't ask her any personal questions.

She made her way around the diner taking orders and going back to the counter to give the orders to Dan. She never had to write down any orders—she was a natural at the job! As the day came to a end, she counted her tips. She had a few dollars, which made her happy. Dan told her that he would give her a paycheck on Friday.

The next day, as Sara was getting ready to start her shift, she heard Dan and Anna arguing. Dan was really mad at Anna. He said, "Don't do it again, Anna!" As Anna came out on the floor to work with Sara, she had a red mark on the side of her face, and she had obviously been crying. Anna was a tall, slim lady with blonde hair and blue eyes that just sparkled. She also had a smile that could light up a room. Sara liked her from the start. Anna looked at Sara and said, "He is so jealous. He thinks every man I wait on is flirting with me. We have been married ten years, and he never changes. I have just learned to live with his threats because his bark is worse than his bite."

13

Chapter

Two

$\mathcal{A}$ few weeks had passed, and things were going well for Sara. She was making enough money to pay some of her expenses. She caught on fast at the diner, and she liked all the people who came in and sat at her tables every day. She and Anna had become friends. Dan seemed to be a good man, but he was very jealous of Anna, and they fought a lot. Everyone who came to eat there knew that Dan was very jealous of Anna. There was this one man they called Wade. He was very good looking, and he had an eye for Anna. He would look at her while she was taking his order with love—or lust. He wanted her, and that was very easy to see. Dan would get so mad at Anna every time Wade came to the diner. Anna was nice to him, but she did not return his flirting. Dan finally told Wade to stay out of his diner. One afternoon, Anna went to the bank to get some change for the diner, and she ran into Wade. She stopped to say hello and told him she was sorry for her husband's actions.

As they were talking, Dan was driving down the street. He saw them and assumed they were making a date. When Anna got back to the diner, he was so mad that he quickly flew out of control. They must have argued for hours. As Sara came in the back door later that day, she saw Dan standing in the kitchen looking down at the floor. Anna was lying on the floor with blood all around her. Sara started screaming as Dan turned around and saw her. She looked at him and saw that he had a gun in his hand. Sara ran out the door, screaming for help. She ran so fast that she didn't realize that she had run a whole city block in just a few minutes. Finally, she saw the local cop, Mac, walking his beat. "What's wrong, little lady?" Did something terrible happen?" he asked.

"Please go back to the White Hat Diner because something horrible has happened!" Sara cried.

Mac called for help for Sara because she was so hysterical. When the police got to the diner, Dan was still standing beside Anna's lifeless body. Mac asked Dan what had happened. "I don't know," he cried. "Anna's dead."

The next morning, Sara had been called to come to the police station. Dan had been taken into custody for shooting Anna. The only person who knew anything was Sara, and she didn't know much. The police questioned her several times and kept her for hours. She told the police what she saw and that Dan was very jealous of Anna. The police finally told Sara she could go home for the night but that she shouldn't leave town. She was so frightened as she thought, *What have I done, coming to this town?* She started to cry as she walked back to the apartment, tears running down her face. *What will I do for a job? They will have to close the diner.* She got so upset that she finally had to sit down on a bench.

As she sat there looking out across the river, she heard a voice say, "Are you okay?" She looked up to see a nice-looking man looking at her.

"Yes, I am. I think so."

"Is there anything I can do?"

"No, I just had a bad day."

"Aren't you the girl who works at the diner?"

"Yes, I have seen you in there."

"Boy, that is terrible what happened. Did Dan really shoot Anna?" Sara asked the man if he knew Dan and Anna.

"I had lunch in there a few times, but that's all," he replied.

"That is why you are so upset, isn't it?"

"Yes, but I can't talk about it. The police have been asking me questions."

"Oh, I am sorry. I won't ask any more questions. By the way, my name is Warren."

"I am Sara."

"Can I walk you the rest of the way home? You look like you need some company."

As they walked, Sara asked Warren where he was from. He told her he was from Eastern Kentucky. "I am in the army and just came into town to see my sister," he said. "She lives over on Court Avenue."

"That is where I live with my sister," Sara said.

Warren was a real cute guy. He had black, wavy hair and blue eyes. Not to tall, but he walked like he was someone important. *That must be how the army teaches them*, Sara thought.

They walked up the stairs to the apartment. "Here is where I live, number 3," Sara said.

Warren said that his sister lived in number 6. Sara thanked him for the walk home. He said, "I hope I will see you again before I leave town." Sara opened the door and went inside.

The next day she got up early. There was a knock on the door. It was Sergeant Mac from the police department. He told her that Dan had confessed to killing Anna, but that there would still be a trial and she would have to testify to what she saw. Sara wondered if she should tell Mac she was only a kid and just about to turn fourteen. She didn't say anything because she figured she would cross that bridge when the time came. For now, she needed to get another job. Sergeant Mac said that it would be a while before the case went to trial and reminded her to not leave town.

Allie told Sara she had seen a sign in the drugstore for help wanted. Sara stopped in there to see if they would hire her. Mr. Martin ran the drugstore. Sara walked up to the soda fountain. She heard a voice say, "Hi there, Sara." She turned around to see Warren standing there talking to the man behind the counter.

"Oh, hi, Warren."

"Mr. Martin, this is my friend Sara," Warren said.

Sara looked Mr. Martin right in the face and said, "Hi, I need a job."

Mr. Martin laughed and said, "Yes, you do."

"Yes, I mean, I want to apply for the job."

"Can you make an ice-cream soda?"

"I can if you show me."

"That sounds good enough for me. Be here in the morning. I think you can learn the job without any problems." Mr. Martin then turned. "Nice talking to you, Warren," he said and then went to the back room. Sara and Warren stood there looking at each other.

Sara said, "I can't believe I got that job." They walked out the door together.

Sara couldn't help but notice how good looking Warren was, and she couldn't keep her eyes off of him. "Do you want to go for a walk?" Warren asked.

"Sure, that would be nice."

As they walked and talked, Sara knew he liked the way she looked. When he looked at her, she felt warm all over. As they were walking, his hand touched hers, and her heart began to pound.

"How old are you, Sara?" he asked.

"Old enough," she told him.

She was not going to tell him her age because she easily looked sixteen. As they stood there on the corner, he leaned over and kissed her on the lips, and she kissed him back. She had never kissed anyone like that before. As Warren pulled back, he said,

"I am sorry. I should not have done that. I'd better go. I've got to meet my sister at 6 o'clock." So off he went, and Sara stood there in a daze for a couple of minutes. Her heart was still pounding.

The next day, she started her job at the soda fountain. She could not keep from thinking about Warren. She wondered if this was what falling in love was like.

Things were going well. She had been working a few months now and was making enough money to help with the rent. Sara had met a real nice girl named Patricia, and they were thinking about getting a room together. It was time she let Allie and Chuck have their apartment back. Patricia worked at the big factory in town. She and Sara had met a month ago. Patricia came in every day after work to get cigarettes and a soda. She was a nice girl. Her boyfriend was overseas in the navy. Sara had met a few guys but none like Warren. It had been several months since she had seen him. She guessed he must have gone back to the army. She dreamed about him every night. She had fallen in love with him. Patricia worked with his sister, Evelyn, who was a very dominating girl. Patricia didn't like her much and said she was too bossy and was a real witch. But Sara said she had not met her so she wasn't going to say anything about her.

As Sara was closing up the soda fountain, she felt like someone was watching her. As she looked up, she couldn't believe her eyes. It was Warren, standing there with a smile on his face. "Hey, Brown Eyes!" he said.

Sara ran around the counter and threw her arms around him. "Where have you been? I have missed you so much! You came into my life, and then you just dropped out of sight," she cried.

"Didn't you get my message?" he asked. "I told my sister to tell you I had to go back to Texas and I would see you when I got back."

"I never heard from your sister, and I have never met her."

"She was supposed to tell you."

As they held each other in their arms, Warren said, "Let's get out of here." Sara told Mr. Martin good night, and off they went. As they walked down the street, Warren said, "My sister has gone home to Kentucky for a few days. Do you want to go to her place where we can be alone to talk? I have so much I want to tell you, Sara."

"I am getting ready to move out of my sister's apartment next week," Sara said. "I am going to share a place with my friend Patricia. A little apartment over on Spring Street. It will be nice to be on my own. Patricia works nights over at the factory so that way we won't be in each other's way all the time."

As they went in the apartment, Sara noticed how nice it was. "Your sister must do pretty well," she said.

"Yes, she has worked up here for a couple of years. Her husband is coming home from the army in a few months."

They sat down on the sofa, and as he lit a cigarette, Warren asked her if she wanted something to drink. He turned on the radio, and Sara told him that was a nice song. Warren laid his cigarette down, pulled Sara close to him, and began to kiss her just like she had dreamed about—soft and long kisses with such passion. "I missed you so much, Sara," he said. "From the first time I saw you, I knew I wanted you."

Sara's heart was pounding. "I love you, Warren," she said.

"I love you, too," he said as they kissed again. He pulled her close and began to kiss her neck and caress her.

She jumped up and said, "I can't do this."

"Okay, okay, you're right," Warren said. "Please don't leave. We will just sit here and talk."

Sara had never been with a guy. She was not ready for all of this. She wanted to be married before she went "all the way." She knew Warren was older and had probably had lots of girls, but she wasn't going to be "just another girl." She knew all about sex. Where she came from, girls married at fourteen all the time. Warren had said he would be in town for a few days, but then he would have to leave again for a few months.

The next day, Warren came into the drugstore with a tall blonde-haired girl. "Sara, I want you to meet Evelyn," he said. They spoke to each other. "I want you two to spend some time together while I am gone and get to know each other."

They both agreed. Sara didn't think she was real friendly but hopefully she would be friendly later. You could tell that Warren looked up to his sister.

Sara and Warren spent as much time together as they could until it was time for him to leave again. They held each other and kissed. Warren said, "I love you, Brown Eyes, and I only have eyes for you. I will get back as soon as I can." It was a tough time as it was the end of WWII, and times were crazy. Soldiers were coming and going everywhere.

Chapter

Three

*T*hree months had passed, and the trial was just about over. Sara had testified, and they were sending the jury out. So many people had taken the stand and told how jealous Dan was of Anna. It was not premeditated; he just lost control when she said she was divorcing him, and he got the gun and shot her in a rage of anger. He was found guilty and was sent to the penitentiary.

Sara was so glad to have that behind her. She saw Dan one time after the trial, and he said that he was sorry for what he had done and what he put her through. Sara never heard from him after that day.

Several months passed. Sara and Patricia were busy getting a picnic lunch ready. They both had a day and night off from work, and they were going to the park. Sara had not heard from Warren for several months. Evelyn always said he was doing fine. Sara and Patricia went to the park and spread their blanket on the ground. They both needed some time to relax. Sara was so lonely for Warren. All she could think about was their last night together before he left to go back to the army. They were so in love, and she had never been in love before. Her heart started pounding just thinking about his lips kissing her. Sara had no experience with lovemaking, and she had never been with anyone. Warren knew that, so he was very gentle with her. Sara had not planned to be with a man until she was married, but she loved Warren so much that it just happened. Sara was okay with it because Warren said they would get married soon.

As Sara lay on the blanket, she daydreamed about Warren. It had been several months since he had been back, and she had only heard from him once. He was supposed to write his sister, and she would let Sara know when he would be home, but his sister didn't seem to like Sara very much. She didn't like Warren to have a girlfriend. Evelyn was very selfish when it came to Warren. She was always telling him what to do.

Suddenly Sara felt like someone was watching her. She opened her eyes and standing over her was Warren. She jumped straight up into his arms and started to cry. "I love you, I love you, and I am so glad you are here!" she cried.

They kissed for a long time. "You'd better come up for air," Patricia said.

"Warren, let's go to the apartment because I have so much to tell you," Sara said.

They picked up the blanket and started back. Patricia said, "You go on without me because I have something to do." Sara was glad to get some time alone with Warren.

The time with Warren was wonderful. They talked about what he would do when he got out of the army. "Maybe you would marry me and we can go back to Kentucky," he said. Sara said that sounded wonderful, but then Warren warned, "But don't say anything to Evelyn about getting married. She tells me all the time that I don't need to be married because I can't take care of myself. She tries to run my life."

"I can see that," said Sara.

The days and weeks passed fast. Sara and Warren spent every minute they could together. Sara had to work because she had to make her rent payment. Warren told Sara he was being sent back to Texas in a few weeks. Her heart was broken. It was so far away! "But," Warren said, "I will send you a train ticket, and you can come out there and see me. Maybe we will get married."

The word *married* was music to Sara's ears. She wanted to marry Warren.

The day came to say goodbye again. But at least this time, she knew she would be going to Texas to see him in a few months. They said their goodbyes with lots of kissing and tears. As Warren was getting on the train, he said again, "Don't let Evelyn know about our plans." Sara said okay. She watched the train pull out of the station even though she had tears in her eyes. Sara wished he hadn't asked her to keep their plan a secret. She wanted to tell everyone. But she *would* tell her best friend, Patricia, because they shared everything.

As she walked back to the apartment, the wind began to blow. Fall was in the air, and her heart was heavy. *How will I ever find my way to Texas?*

Chapter

Four

The weeks had passed as Sara kept herself busy working.
She ran into Evelyn at the drugstore. "Have you heard from Warren?" Evelyn asked. Sara said yes.

Evelyn laughed and said, "You and half a dozen others. He
has a girl in every state!" She was laughing as she walked away.

Sara didn't like what she said, but she knew that Evelyn was
a mean person and she didn't want Warren to have a girlfriend.
Sara couldn't understand why Evelyn was like that, but she knew
Warren loved her and they were going to have a life together.

Thanksgiving was almost here, and the first snow had fallen.
Sara was walking home from work, and the snow was getting
down in her shoes. Her coat wasn't heavy enough for the cold
weather, but she would be at the apartment soon and she could
get warm. Sara was hoping that Patricia had gotten home and
had the coffee pot going. A cup of hot coffee would warm her up.
As she walked up the stairs, she saw that there was something in
her mailbox. She got so excited that she began to shake all over.
It was a letter from Warren! Sara ran into the apartment yelling,
"I got a letter! I know this is the one I have been waiting for!"

Patricia tried to calm Sara down. "You won't know unless you read it," she said.

Sara asked Patricia to read it to her because she was too excited to read. Patricia took the letter and began to read it: "My dearest Brown Eyes, I hope you are well. Here is your ticket. I can't wait to see you. Love, Warren."

"I am going to Texas, and I can't believe it!" Sara exclaimed. Patricia said that it was a two-day trip by train. "I know it is a long way, but I have to go," Sara said. "I think we are going to get married."

Patricia looked at Sara and said, "You *think*."

"I am going no matter what, because he wants me to come to him, and I am going." Sara knew it would be a hard trip for her, but once she got on the train, she wouldn't have to get off until she got to San Antonio. And Warren would be there waiting for her. It took a few days to get things ready for the trip. She had worked at the drugstore for over a year with hardly any time off, so she knew she could have a week off. Patricia worked nights at the factory, and she told the drugstore manager that she would help them out during the day if they needed her. She was a great friend to Sara.

The day had come for Sara to leave, and she was very excited. Patricia took her to the train station, and they said their goodbyes. "I will see you when you get back. Be careful," Patricia said.

Sara boarded the train with her small suitcase and a happy heart. She was going to see the man she loved—maybe even the man she would marry. Sara found her seat. She looked so nice in her little brown suit and hat that matched her heels. She looked like she was twenty instead of sixteen. Sara never told her correct age. She had been on her own since she was thirteen so she had grown up fast. She didn't miss being a child. It wasn't fun, and she had hated school. She had no nice clothes to wear so she wouldn't go to school. She had not been back to the third-grade class in the one-room schoolhouse since the day the kids had first made fun of her dress. Her mother had made it out of a flour sack. Her sister didn't seem to mind the teasing, but Sara said that no one was going to make fun of her again, so she never went back. She went into town and began to work for a lady. She saved her money, bought two store dresses, and never wore a flour-sack dress again.

The train was full of people, and Sara was getting tired. She had packed a lunch for the trip. She knew she didn't have a lot of money to spend on food so she packed her own. She was sitting by the window. Sara watched as the sun began to set. What a beautiful sight. She watched as the sun set and night came. All she could think about was being in Warren's arms. She closed her eyes to sleep for a while.

The sun shining through the window woke Sara up for a few minutes. She forgot for a moment that she was on a train going to San Antonio, Texas. The pains in her stomach told her it was morning. The conductor came walking by and said that they would be stopping in Oklahoma City to pick up some passengers, "so feel free to get out and stretch your legs and use the facilities." That sounded good to Sara.

As she was going into the train station, a nice older lady dressed in a beautiful blue suit said good morning. She was very tall and so nice looking. She was carrying a basket with her, and it had a pretty ribbon tied on it. Sara walked around for a couple of minutes, not believing she was actually in Oklahoma. In a few hours she would be in Texas, and she could hardly wait!

As she was walking back to her seat, she saw the nice lady sitting in the seat next to her. She sat down and said hello again. "I am Sara, and I am going to San Antonio."

The lady smiled and said, "I am Mrs. Banks, and I am going there, too. We have about eight more hours to travel."

Sara was trying to think what time it would be when she arrived in San Antonio—it would be about 5 in the afternoon. Mrs. Banks asked if Sara had someone to meet her at the station. "Oh, yes," said Sara, "I am going to meet the man I am going to marry."

"Well, congratulations to you! That's very exciting."

Sara asked Mrs. Banks why she was going to San Antonio. "I am a teacher on the reservation for the Indian children," she replied.

"That's a wonderful job," said Sara.

As Sara looked up, she noticed that many of the passengers had left the train car and had gone to the dining car for their breakfast. Sara had her own food so she opened up her brown bag. She had one biscuit and an apple left. Mrs. Banks opened up her basket, and Sara couldn't believe her eyes. She had fruit, a loaf of bread, smoked ham, and a big piece of pie. Mrs. Banks watched Sara eat her food in about five minutes and noticed that Sara was still hungry. Mrs. Banks said she had plenty and offered some food to Sara. Sara said thank you and then enjoyed the best-tasting ham she had ever had. They finished their food and settled back into their seats for the rest of the trip.

Sara had a spool of red ribbon in her purse. She pulled it out and started tying pretty little knots to make a necklace. She had made them before, and everyone always remarked how cute they were. It helped to pass the time. Mrs. Banks had a small book she was reading. Sara wished she could read a book like that. It made her sad to think about that and ashamed to think someone might find out that she could not read. She had to keep this secret from Warren. Sara had learned how to hide it very well. Sara was able to write her name. She was very clever because she had been able to keep her secret from everyone; she didn't want anyone to ever know that she could not read.

The hours soon passed, and Sara heard the conductor yell, "Next stop San Antonio!" and her heart almost stopped. She was so excited that she could not stay in her seat. The train began to slow down and then came to a stop. The jerk of the train knocked her back into her seat and woke up Mrs. Banks. Sara said, "We are here!" with such excitement that Mrs. Banks laughed.

"Sara dear, here is my address if you need anything while you are here."

"It was a pleasure meeting you, Mrs. Banks."

"I wish you the best, Sara, and always stay as sweet and so full of life as you are today and may God bless you."

Sara gave her a hug and headed off the train.

Sara started walking into the station looking for Warren. Her heart was just about to come out of her chest. *Where was Warren?* About an hour had passed, and she was beginning to get worried. She walked up to the counter and asked how far it was to the army post. A nice-looking older gentleman looked up and said it was about twenty miles away. As Sara turned to walk away, she heard someone say, "Hey, good looking, do you need a ride?" She turned around fast, and there stood Warren with the biggest smile on his face!

Sara screamed with joy as she threw her arms around him. "I didn't think you were coming!" she cried.

"I am sorry I was late getting off the post, but I got three days off, and we are going to spend every minute together," he told her.

Warren had rented them a room in town. Sara was so thrilled to be with Warren because she loved him so much. Warren said, "Let's get going. We have a lot to talk about, and I can't wait to get you alone." As they drove away from the train station, Sara told Warren that this was the happiest day of her life. He put his arm around her, pulled her close, and said, "I love you, Sara."

The next morning, Sara woke up before Warren. She lay there in bed looking at his sweet, boy-like face and his black, wavy hair. He was so handsome. She was wondering if they might get married that day. She hoped so after a night like they had. They had made love all night long. She wished it would have been her honeymoon. Sara had never been with anyone before Warren and he was ten years older so she knew he had other women in his life. But he told her she was the only one he ever wanted to marry.

Sara and Warren spent the next few days having a wonderful time. As they walked down the street to the little diner on the corner, Warren held Sara's hand, and then he suddenly slipped something on her finger. She pulled her hand up to see what it was. Warren had put a pretty little silver band on her finger. "What is this?" she exclaimed.

"It's a ring. What did you think it was?"

"But what does this mean? Are we getting married?"

"Not today, but someday. I love you, Sara, and I want you to have this ring so you know how much you mean to me."

Sara loved the ring, but she was disappointed and started to cry.

"Don't cry," Warren said. "When I get back to Indiana, we will get married. I want you to meet my parents—they will love you."

Sara thought, *Your sister doesn't like me, and she won't like you getting married.* Evelyn was so domineering that she didn't want Warren to have a life of his own. Warren would be out of the army in a few months, and he had a job lined up in Indiana so Sara was happy about that. Warren said he thought Evelyn and Brian would be moving back to Kentucky soon. Sara wanted Evelyn to get as far away from her and Warren as she could.

The next couple of days just flew by, but they were wonderful days. Now it was time to go to the train station. Sara started to cry, and said, "I don't want to leave you, Warren."

"But just think—in a few months I will be in Indiana and out of the army. Then we will have all the time we want to be together." Warren put his arms around Sara, held her so close, kissed her, and said, "I will think of you every minute we are apart. I only have eyes for you, my love." Warren was so sweet, and Sara knew it would be all right. They kissed, and she said, "I love you," as she got on the train. Sara waved goodbye to Warren as the tears ran down her cheeks. Warren stayed on the train platform until the train was out of sight. As Sara found her seat, the tears were still coming. She knew she had to pull herself together. After all, she would see him again in about six months. Sara knew they would get married when he came home.

Sara settled back in her seat for the long train ride home. Sara closed her eyes so she could relive all the wonderful times they had spent together the last three days.

Sara opened her eyes to see the conductor looking at her. "Are you all right, young lady?" he asked.

"Yes, I am just fine. Why do you ask?"

"You have been asleep for a good while."

"I was tired. Why are we stopping?"

"It is time to fuel up and pick up more passengers." Sara got up and stretched her legs. "You have time to go into the station if you want." So Sara went in the station to look around and freshen up. As she walked off the train, she saw so many solders. Sara couldn't keep from thinking about Warren. She guessed these soldiers were going home to be with their wives and girlfriends. Sara just kept thinking, *Six months, and Warren will be coming home to me.* As she was washing her hands and face, she heard the train whistle blow. *Oh, I've got to hurry and get back on the train.*

Sara hurried to find her seat and to get comfortable for the rest of the trip home because it would be another five hours. Sara closed her eyes to rest.

Sara woke to see the conductor standing over her. "Young lady, we are pulling into the train station. I think this is where you get off."

"Oh my, I have been asleep for a long time." Sara gathered up her things and headed off the train. It was about three in the morning. She had a few blocks to walk to get to her apartment.

Sara was tired and hungry when she reached her apartment. She unlocked the door quietly so she would not wake up Patricia. She put her suitcase down and took her shoes off. Sara headed for the little kitchen to see if there was any food. There was a small plate of biscuits. Sara was about to pop one in her mouth when Patricia came around the corner.

"I knew I heard something! Welcome home, and how was the trip?"

"It was wonderful. Look what Warren gave me!" Sara held up her hand to show Patricia the silver band.

"Oh, it's beautiful. You got married!"

"No, we didn't, but we will when Warren gets here in a few months."

Sara and Patricia had a cup of coffee and talked for a while. Finally Patricia said, "Sara, you had better get to bed because they are expecting you to be at work in the morning at the drugstore."

Morning came faster than Sara wanted it to. She was up after only a few hours of sleep. She got her bath and a bite to eat and was off to work. Patricia was able to sleep in because she didn't have to be at work until 3:00 in the afternoon at the factory.

Sara walked in the door at the drugstore. Mr. Martin was glad to see her. "How was your trip?"

"It was great."

"How was Warren? I hope he made an honest woman out of you."

Sara just raised her hand up without thinking.

"Well, congratulations!"

Sara grabbed her apron, got behind the soda fountain, and started to work. She hardly had time to think because she was so busy.

Chapter

Five

Time passed fast. It had been about six weeks, and she had not heard from Warren. When she saw Evelyn walking home from work, she said hi. Evelyn asked if she had heard from Warren.

"Yes, I have," Sara lied.

"Well, did you know that he has been in the hospital?"

Sara's heart sank. "He didn't tell me that."

"His stomach gives him trouble a lot, and he had some tests done. His ulcers are active again."

"I will be so glad when he comes home for good. He has a job waiting for him here in town."

"Oh, he will go back to Kentucky because he won't stay up here. I guess you two are going to get married."

Before Sara could say anything, Evelyn walked away laughing. Sara was so mad. Evelyn was so mean. *Why didn't Warren tell me he had been sick?* she wondered.

The next day there was a letter in her mailbox from Warren. Sara was so excited. She opened it up and tried to read it but she could not make out the words. Sara lay in her bed holding onto the letter, crying and waiting for Patricia to get home from the night shift. The door opened and Sara jumped up and ran to Patricia.

"Warren has been sick! Please read this to me."

Patricia said, "Stop crying and calm down. Did it say that he was sick in the letter?"

"No, Evelyn told me. Patricia, I can't read. I am sorry I didn't tell you, but I am so embarrassed that I never learned to read. Please read the letter to me."

Patricia read: "*Dear Brown Eyes, Sorry I have not written but have been in the hospital with my stomach and haven't felt well. I am okay now and looking forward to seeing you in a few months. Love, Warren.*"

"How can you get by without reading, Sara?"

"I just memorize things and fake it." Sara started to cry.

"It will be okay, Sara. Maybe I can teach you to read."

"It is not the reading. I feel so sick that I can't eat. I think I might be pregnant."

Patricia said, "Oh, no. It can't be. What in the world are you going to do?"

"Well, Warren said we would get married when he gets home. He will be home in three months. We will go to the doctor this week and find out."

Sara and Patricia walked out of the doctor's office. "Well, I guess I can keep this a secret until Warren gets in town. No one is to know because it can't get back to Evelyn before I tell Warren. He would be mad."

Sara was already two months pregnant. That Texas trip did it. Sara knew Warren would be happy, and everything would be just fine. They would get a place to live, he would get his job, and they would have a happy life!

Sara was busy working behind the soda fountain at Martin's Drugstore, and she never missed a day. Mr. Martin said he thought his customers came in just to see Sara because she always had a smile for everyone. She could also make a great soda. Sara was able to keep her pregnancy a secret. Patricia was the only one who knew.

Sara had finished her day's work, and it was about 7 o'clock. Mr. Martin said, "See you tomorrow, Sara, and have a good evening." It was almost dark as she started down the street. Sara heard someone whistle behind her, and as she turned around, there stood Warren. She was so surprised that she almost fainted. Warren grabbed her up in his arms and kissed her. "I missed you so much that I had to come to town a week early to see you," he said.

As Warren was holding Sara in his arms, he said, "Brown Eyes, I think you have gained a couple of pounds!" Sara started to cry. "Don't cry! I am just kidding. You are no bigger than a pound of soap." That made Sara laugh. They started walking down the street to Sara's apartment.

"Are you out of the army now?"

"Yes, darling, Uncle Sam is finished with me. Now we can start our life together, just you and me. I don't want Evelyn to know I am in town. I want a few days alone with you."

"Patricia is working a double shift so we have some time alone. We have a lot to talk about."

As they walked up the stairs, Warren couldn't keep his hands off Sara. He said, "I have missed you so much. I can't wait to have you alone."

Sara stopped and gave Warren a long, passionate kiss and said, "I love you, Warren, but I need to tell you something first."

"You can tell me in bed."

"No, I can't, so please sit down on the sofa."

"Okay, what could be so important?"

Sara took a deep breath and said, "Remember what a wonderful time we had in San Antonio?"

"Yes."

"Well, I am five months pregnant."

Warren just looked at her like he could see through her. "You're what?!"

Sara started to cry as she said, "I am pregnant. I don't want to be pregnant and not be married."

"Does anyone know?" Warren asked.

"Only Patricia and, of course, the doctor."

"Well, you're wearing the ring so maybe people will think we are married," Warren said. "We will work this out. A baby! I'm going to be a daddy!"

"Then is it okay, and you are happy?"

"Sure, Brown Eyes. You know I love you, and it is fine."

They held each other in their arms. Sara felt so much better. Warren was going to work everything out.

A few days passed, and Warren said, "I need to go and check on my job and see Evelyn. I will see you later tonight at the drugstore when you get off work. We will catch a movie." Warren blew her a kiss as he walked away. Sara didn't want to go to the movies. She wanted to get married and get a place for her and Warren and start their life together.

Sara was closing up the drugstore at almost 8 o'clock. Mr. Martin said, "I thought Warren was picking you up."

"He is supposed to. We are going to the movies."

"I am going that way, so I will walk with you. Maybe he meant he would meet you at the movie house."

"Maybe," said Sara, but she had a sick feeling that something was wrong. Mr. Martin walked with her to the movie house. He left Sara waiting for Warren in front of the theater. The movie was starting at 8:30. Mr. Martin said, "See you tomorrow," as he walked down Spring Street toward his house.

Sara waited about thirty minutes and then started walking home. She cried all the way home because she felt like she was going to die. She kept thinking that Warren hadn't shown up because he didn't want to marry her. Her heart was broken, but as she reached the apartment stairs she had calmed down a little. She opened the door to the apartment and there stood Warren talking to Patricia. "Where have you been?" she exclaimed. "I was waiting for you at the Starlight Theater."

"I forgot—I thought we were to meet here."

Patricia said, "I will see you all later." Sara noticed a disturbed look on Patricia's face. She wondered what Warren had asked her.

Warren said, "Let's sit down and talk, Sara. I have been talking to Evelyn. I love you, Sara, but I can't be a father. Evelyn said I can't even take care of myself."

"I thought you loved me."

"I do, but what would we do with a baby?"

"We would be a family, and we would love it and take care of it."

"Evelyn said you should just get rid of it."

"Why don't you tell Evelyn to stay out of our life? I am telling you right now, Warren, that I will never get rid of this child. It will be born in three months with or without you."

"I really do love you, Sara, but I don't think I can be a father."

"Just go, get out of here, and go to Evelyn and leave me alone." She pushed him toward the door and then slammed it. She was heartsick and so angry. *I will never give up my baby. If Warren doesn't want it, I will make it on my own.* Sara cried herself to sleep that night.

The next morning, Sara was fixing a cup of coffee when Patricia came in from working the night shift. Patricia walked over and put her arms around Sara. "I am so sorry about you and Warren," she said.

"He just doesn't want to be a father, and he said that Evelyn was so mad at him. Evelyn said it probably wasn't even his baby. That Evelyn is so mean. Why does he listen to her? He is the only one. I gave myself to him in love and because I knew we were going to get married. How can he do this?"

"What will you do, Sara?"

"Well, we are going to get out of this town and find a place to live and get a job. I have been taking care of myself for three years so I guess I will keep on. I just will have a baby to take care of."

A few days passed, and Sara and Patricia were packing their clothes to move. All they had were their clothes because the apartment was furnished. They could ride the bus to the next town. It was a little bigger and had lots of place to work. Sara was still not showing her pregnancy very much. She could get a job waiting tables.

There was a knock at the door. Patricia opened the door, and there stood Warren. Sara turned around and said, "I don't want to talk to you."

"But, Sara, I just had to see you one more time."

Patricia said, "You two talk, and I will take a walk."

Sara was firm. "Warren, there is nothing left to be said. You made your choice."

"But, Sara, I love you."

"That's not enough, Warren. We made this baby out of love, but you don't want it, so that means you don't want me, either. Get out of my life, and leave me alone. My heart is broken, but this baby and I will be just fine." She pushed him toward the door and slammed it shut. She fell down in the middle of the floor thinking she might just die from the awful pain in her heart. Sara realized she wouldn't die because she was too mad to die.

Chapter

Six

The next day Sara and Patricia were on the bus headed for Ludlow. It was a nice little town on the river. They got off the bus on State Street, and they started walking down Main Street. There were lots of houses that just rented rooms. One of the girls that Patricia worked with at the factory had given her the name of a lady that might help them out. Patricia had lost her job, so neither one of them had much money. They walked about twelve blocks before they found the place they were looking for. It was a big three-story house that needed painting. They knocked on the door. An older, heavyset woman with gray hair said, "May I help you?"

Sara said, "We are looking for a Miss Davis."

She said, "It looks like you need a room, or either you just like carrying around your suitcase."

"Yes, we need a room, but we need to know the cost. We just got in town and we don't have jobs yet."

"Well, come on in, and take a load off your feet."

Sara liked this woman. She showed them a room. It was small with two twin beds, one dresser, and a small chair in the corner, and it was clean. "How much is the room?" she asked.

"Ten dollars a week, but you share the bathroom with the four other girls that live here. I cook the meals. Nothing fancy, but it is hot. You have to help clean up the kitchen."

Sara told Patricia that this would work. Sara told Miss Davis that they would take the room.

"One more thing," she said. "I don't allow any men in the rooms."

The next day Sara was up and out of the house. She had to get a job fast. There was a cafeteria down the street. Miss Davis told her to ask for Frances. As soon as Sara walked in the cafeteria, a lady walked up to her and said, "You must be Sara. Can you wait tables?"

"Yes, ma'am."

"Then go to work."

Miss Davis was so good to Sara. About two months had passed, and things were going well. Sara tried not to think of Warren, but it was hard to not think of him with the baby growing in her. Sara decided that she would just tell people that her husband had been killed in a car crash while she was pregnant. No one knew she was pregnant except Patricia, but she was beginning to show. After all, the baby was due in about a month. She needed to find a doctor real soon.

One evening Sara was washing the dishes for Miss Davis. When she turned around, Miss Davis was right behind her, and Sara wiped her hands on her belly. Miss Davis asked, "When is your baby due?"

It shocked Sara so much she couldn't answer for a minute.

"Well, are you going to have a baby, or did you swallow a watermelon?"

"Oh, yes, I am. I think she will be born next month."

"You know she is a girl?"

"Oh, yes, I know it is a girl."

"Where is the father, Sara?"

"Oh, he died in a car crash a few months ago."

Miss Davis didn't say anything except that Sara needed to see the doctor. "I don't have a doctor."

"Well, we will go tomorrow. I will get you a doctor."

The next day Sara met the doctor. He was a nice man, and he said that she looked healthy, but that she needed to eat a little more. The baby should be born in about four weeks. Sara told Dr. Silver that she didn't have any money and that her husband had died. "I will only be able to pay you a little money at a time. I do have a job at the cafeteria, so as soon as I have the baby, I will go back to work. Miss Davis said she would help with the baby."

Dr. Silver said, "That will be fine, Sara." He gave Sara some papers to read and told her to go to the hospital when she went in labor and he would see her there. As Dr. Silver walked away, he knew this young girl was on her own, but she had a strong will and lots of guts. If anyone could pull this off, she could. Miss Davis had told him she was determined to keep her baby, and he was going to make sure she did.

Well, the weeks passed, and Sara worked every day from morning to night. She was having a lot of back pain, and she told Miss Davis that she thought it was time to go to the hospital. "I will come when I can, Sara," Miss Davis told her.

The cab driver headed for the hospital. Sara said to stop by the coat factory first. "I have to tell my friend Patricia."

"Are you sure? Because I don't want a baby born in my cab." So, the cab stopped at the factory, and Sara ran in to tell Patricia the baby was coming soon. Patricia told her boss that she needed to go with Sara because she had no one else. So off they went. Patricia knew she could fill out the papers for Sara. No one knew that Sara could not read except Patricia. Sara kept that secret to herself. She could write her name but not too well.

They made it to the hospital, and a few hours later, Sara had a beautiful baby girl. Dr. Silver said he had never delivered such a beautiful baby. Black hair and brown eyes. Sara was a natural mother. She knew just what to do. Dr. Silver knew Sara would be a good mother. The nuns at the hospital fell in love with Sara and her baby. They brought the baby a nice big basket because they knew Sara had nothing.

The day they left the hospital, Dr. Silver came in to tell Sara goodbye and good luck. Sara said, "I will come by and pay you some money next week. I am going to go to work tomorrow."

"Sara, you don't owe me a thing."

Sara started to cry and she tried to speak.

"No, Sara, I just want you and your baby to have a good life."

"Thank you, Dr. Silver."

"Oh, there was a long-distance phone call this morning from some man who wanted to know if you were giving the baby up. I told him no."

"Thank you, Dr. Silver."

Chapter

Seven

$\mathcal{A}$ few weeks passed, and Sara was back to work. It was real hard working all day and getting up in the night with Baby Molly. Sara loved her baby so much. She looked like Warren, and Sara tried not to think about him because it hurt too bad. She knew that was who had called the hospital. *How dare he think I would give up my baby*, she thought.

Sara was in the kitchen washing out clothes for the baby when she heard a voice say, "Milkman." She turned around to see a nice-looking man standing there with milk in his hands. "Hi there, just going to put the milk in the icebox," he said.

Miss Davis walked in and said, "Hi, Mr. Preston. Be sure and leave an extra quart of milk. I got to fatten up this little lady. She just had a baby a few weeks ago. This is Sara."

Mr. Preston said, "Hello! Let's see that baby!"

Sara was always ready to show off Molly because she was a beautiful baby. Sara came out with Molly in her arms and said, "Here she is."

He pulled the blanket back and said, "She is a pretty one. She looks like her mama."

Sara blushed.

"You are both pretty girls. Got to get back to work. See you the next time. Take care of that baby."

"What a nice man, that milkman," Miss Davis said. "He is a good man. He is raising three kids by himself. He has had some bad luck. His wife died a few months ago. She was only thirty-five years old. Mr. Preston has had such a hard time getting good help. The two older ones help with the younger one. Everyone has a hard time now and then in life."

Sara was rocking Molly in the big chair that Miss Davis let her use. As Sara rocked Molly and looked into her innocent face, she could not keep from wondering, *What in the world am I going to do? I have the job at the cafeteria. It's not a lot of money, but enough to buy milk for Molly and pay Miss Davis.* A few people had asked about Molly's father. Sara was sticking to her story that he was killed in a car accident, and that was all she was going to say. His name was on Molly's birth certificate, and Molly had his name.

A few days had passed, and Sara was back at the cafeteria. She was busy cleaning off the tables when Francis walked over and said there were two men in here this morning asking about her. Sara turned around fast and asked who they were. Her heart was about to jump out of her chest.

"The dark-haired one asked if you'd had your baby. I told them yes and that you had a pretty little girl."

Sara knew that must be Warren. "Please don't tell anyone about me."

Francis said, "I figure it was some of your family. I don't have any family around here, and if I did, they wouldn't be in here asking about me."

Sara was upset and Francis knew it. All Sara could think about was what if they wanted to take Molly away from her. Sara finished her shift and headed back to the apartment. She was thinking to herself, *They will have to kill me before they get Molly. Warren didn't want us before. Why is he here now? He will mess everything up.* As she got closer to the apartment, she saw Warren and his cousin standing out in front of the building. Her heart dropped. Sara started to run the other way, and then she thought, *No, I am going to tell him to get out of my life.* She just hoped and prayed that he did not tell anyone who he was.

As she walked up to him, he said, "You look great, Sara. Surprised to see me?"

"Yes, I am. What are you doing here?"

"I wanted to see you and the baby. You remember my cousin, Tommy."

"Yes. Hi there. Why do you want to see the baby? You didn't want her, if I remember. I want you to leave, Warren. I am getting on with my life. You didn't want us, so you leave now and don't you ever try to see us again."

"But Sara, Evelyn wanted me to see what the baby looked like."

The hair on the back of Sara's neck stood up. She was so angry at that remark. "The baby looks just like you, Warren."

"I know that she is mine and I will never get to know her. I am sorry, Sara."

"Please just go away, Warren. All I want from you is to leave me alone. You made your choice, and it is not Molly or me."

"Her name is Molly?"

"Yes."

Warren turned and walked away. Sara stood there on the sidewalk. Her heart was broken into a million pieces. She had fought back the tears so hard that she could hardly swallow. Her heart was in pain, and her head felt like she was going to faint. She knew that if she started to cry, she would never stop. Then she would have to explain what was wrong. Her story had been told, and she wasn't changing it.

Chapter

Eight

$\mathcal{A}$ few weeks had passed, and Sara was trying to move on. She was sweeping off the front porch when the milkman came up the walk. "Hi there," he said. "Looks like you can use a broom."

"Why, of course, anyone can sweep."

"Not the woman I have working at my house. I can't find anyone who knows how to clean a house or cook."

"I can clean and cook, Mr. Preston."

"Are you looking for a job, Sara?"

"Well, yes I am. But I have my baby."

"I need someone to live at my house and take care of my children. That would be a big job for someone with a new baby. Why don't you come to my house and meet my children and see if you want the job?"

"I do need a place to live. It would help us both. I will see you tomorrow afternoon."

Mr. Preston gave her directions on how to get there. It was about twelve blocks away so she could put Molly in the baby buggy and walk up to Elm Street.

Sara could hardly wait to tell Miss Davis what had happened. Miss Davis was thrilled for Sara. "Mr. Preston is a good man, Sara, and he has a nice home and family. He has been through a lot in the last year. I hope it will work out for you."

Sara was so excited but a little nervous, too. She knew she could do the work. It would be hard but she was used to hard work.

As she walked up the front walk, she could see Mr. Preston sitting on the front porch. He was smoking his pipe. The smoke was in a circle around his head. It looked like a halo. "Oh my goodness," She said. "I have been praying for help. Maybe God has sent me an angel." Sara reached the porch. "Come on in, Sara." Molly was sleeping in the buggy, but Sara got her out and carried her in with her.

The house was big and nice, but it needed some work. Mr. Preston said, "These are my children. Jack is fourteen. This is Donna, and she is twelve. Here is Larry, the baby, and he is six. Say hello to Sara. She might take the job as housekeeper."

Jack spoke up and asked, "Can you cook?"

"Yes, I can." Sara noticed that the children were looking her over.

Larry said, "What kind of baby is that?"

"It is a little girl, and her name is Molly. She is only a few weeks old."

"I guess she can't play yet, since she is too little."

Donna asked if she could hold her and Sara said yes. Mr. Preston said to the children, "She sure is a pretty baby."

Jack asked if she cried a lot.

"No, she is a real good baby."

Finally Mr. Preston said, "Let's go out on the porch and talk." Donna handed Molly back to Sara, and as Sara took Molly, she said, "I hope you will come to work here." That made Sara feel good. Sara knew these were good kids.

Sara walked out to the porch, and Mr. Preston said, "Have a seat, Sara." She sat down and began to swing Molly, and it wasn't long before she was asleep. Mr. Preston asked, "What do you think about the job, Sara? I would need for you to start as soon as you can. You would share the room with Donna. It is big enough, and we could put the baby crib in there. I would expect you to keep the house and do the wash and cook the meals. Jack and Donna can help. Larry is too little, and he is having a hard time with his mother not being here. She died last year, and the children have had such a hard time. How do you explain death to children?"

Sara said, "I don't know."

He said, "Life is a funny thing. You never know what it will throw your way. You just have to make the best with what you have, so maybe we can help each other."

Sara said, "Yes. I need a job, and you need a housekeeper, so I will take the job."

"If it gets to be too big of a job, you let me know. I know it is a big job for someone as young as you are and with a new baby."

"Well, I am not that young, and where I come from, you grow up fast. I never got to be a child. I want a better life for Molly. I want her to have a childhood and grow up the right way."

Mr. Preston didn't ask any personal questions. He just said, "I will give you a comfortable place to live while you work for me."

Sara thanked Mr. Preston and said that she would be there the first of the week. She put Molly back in the buggy and headed back downtown to Miss Davis's house.

The next morning, Sara was having a cup of coffee before going to work at the cafeteria. Miss Davis came in the kitchen. Sara said, "I took the job, and I am going to work for Mr. Preston. His kids are nice, and I think I can do a good job. It will be a nice place to live. The kids seemed to like Molly. I am going to start the first of the week. I have to tell them at the cafeteria that I won't be back."

"Slow down, Sara, I know you are excited, but I want you to think about this. Mr. Preston is a good man, and I think you have made a good decision, but remember, he is a man without a wife, and he is only human so just be careful."

"I trust him, and I will be in his daughter's room. I told him I was older than what I am. I have had to lie about my age so much. I am not a lot older than Jack and Donna, but they will never know that. Mr. Preston sure loves babies. He really likes Molly. He said she had the biggest brown eyes he has ever seen. Well, I'd better get out of here, so I can tell them at work that I won't be back. It will be all right because their business has been slow."

Sara was busy cleaning off some tables when Francis came in.

"Good morning, Sara."

"Good morning, Miss Francis. I would like to talk to you when you have a few minutes."

"Let's talk now because things are slow around here."

"I just wanted to thank you for letting me work here, but I have another job that will give me room and board. So, I need to let you know that tomorrow will be my last day."

"Are you going to work for the nice Mr. Preston?"

"Yes, I am."

"Well, I wish you the best. Miss Davis said he offered you a job. It will be hard work, Sara, with three kids to clean up after, but there is not a nicer man in this town. I hope it works out for you. Good luck."

Chapter

———⊰❧⊱———

Nine

The day had come for Sara to move up to Mr. Preston's house. Patricia had helped her get her few things together. Sara had Molly in her basket and one suitcase for the both of them, not a lot to move. She left the baby buggy at Miss Davis's place since they were taking a cab. Miss Davis told Sara that she would bring it up to her one afternoon. Patricia was going to miss Sara and Molly. They had been through a lot, and they were like sisters.

The cab picked them up, and off they went to 1900 Elm Street. Sara was nervous and excited about her new job. The cab pulled up in front of the Preston house. She paid the cab driver the fare, and as she looked up, there stood Jack, Donna, and Larry. They were all trying to get the cab door open. Sara said, "Slow down."

Donna said, "Let me take Molly."

Jack got the suitcase, and Larry was just trying to help. Jack said, "Is this all you have, Sara?"

"Yes, that's it."

They got in the house, and Donna showed Sara where to put her things. They already had the crib in her bedroom. Sara said, "I hope you don't mind sharing your room with us."

53

Donna said, "Not at all! I love babies, and it will be so nice to have a girl in the house."

It didn't take Sara long to put her things away. It was time for Molly's nap. "Can I rock her for you, Sara?"

"Sure, you can."

As Donna rocked Molly, Sara headed out to the kitchen.

It was time to get dinner started. Sara wanted to have dinner on the table when Mr. Preston got home from work. She started checking out the kitchen. It was such a big room. There was a big round table over by the double windows. There was a nice big cabinet with a flour bin and a place to roll out dough for biscuits. There was coffee and lots of food in the cabinet. *I wonder who does the grocery shopping*, Sara thought. There was everything you needed to cook a meal. She looked in the icebox. There was a lot of milk. She loved milk, and she had not had a glass of milk in a long time. She found some ground beef in a package. Sara started putting the meal together. She made meatloaf, mashed potatoes, and some corn.

Sara was busy working in the kitchen when Jack came in. "What smells so good?" he asked. "There has not been anything good come out of this kitchen in a long time. Dad tries to cook. We can eat it, but this smells great."

Sara said, "I have a meatloaf in the oven and some biscuits."

Jack said, "I can hardly wait to eat." He told Sara that the last housekeeper they had could only cook beans, and she would burn them most of the time.

It was just about time for Mr. Preston to come home from work. He got home about 5:30 every night. Donna helped set the table. She put five plates on the table. Sara said no, that she would eat after everyone had finished, and so Donna took her plate off the table.

Sara heard the front door open and heard Larry yell, "Daddy's home! Daddy's home!"

Sara stayed in the kitchen where she felt she belonged. Sara heard Mr. Preston ask, "What smells so good?"

Jack said, "You are not going to believe what Sara has cooked."

"Let's go get washed up for supper."

The kids could hardly wait to get to the table. Mr. Preston said, "It sure looks good, Sara," as the kids sat down. He then said, "Where is your place, Sara?"

"I will eat later."

"Oh, no, you won't. You will eat with us."

About that time, Molly started to cry. "I have to get Molly. I will eat later," Sara said. "You all go ahead and eat."

Mr. Preston got up and went to the cabinet and got out a plate and some silverware and sat Sara down. He walked out of the kitchen and came back in a minute with Molly in his arms. She wasn't crying anymore. Sara said, "I will take her while you eat your supper."

The kids were eating like there was no tomorrow. Jack said, "It sure is good!"

Mr. Preston said, "I have missed holding a little one. She sure is sweet."

They all finished their supper together.

The next morning, Sara got up about five o'clock and made the coffee and started breakfast for Mr. Preston. He was surprised to see her in the kitchen so early. "You didn't have to do this for me, Sara," he said. "I can get by on a cup of coffee. It is the children I need you to take care of."

"I already have your breakfast ready so you might as well eat. I am used to getting up early. Molly has a four o'clock feeding so I was awake."

He told her the breakfast was good, but she should just take care of the children in the morning. "I will be fine," he said.

The weeks and months passed. Sara was settled in, and things were going fine. Sara and Donna had gotten the house organized. Everyone seemed to be adjusting to Sara and Molly. Molly was really growing, and she was such a happy baby.

Chapter

Ten

It was a warm fall evening, Sara had put Molly to bed, and she was sitting on the front porch in the swing. Jack had gone out with his friends, and Donna was spending the night at a girlfriend's house. Larry was lying on the living-room floor looking at his comic books. Mr. Preston came out on the front porch. He saw Sara swinging, her long brown hair blowing in the breeze. Sara noticed he was looking at her. "What is wrong, Mr. Preston?" she asked.

"Nothing is wrong, Sara, but it would be all right for you to call me Richard."

Sara stopped the swing and said, "I can do that if that is what you want."

"May I sit down with you?"

"Sure. Do you like to swing, Mr. Preston, I mean, Richard?"

"Yes, I do."

"I really like my job here, and your children are so wonderful to Molly. They have grown to love Molly, and they are very fond of you, too."

"I hope you don't mind me saying this, Sara, but I have become very fond of you. You are a beautiful young woman. Do you have any plans on how you are going raise Molly on your own?"

"I am just going to do the best that I can do. I have no other choice."

"I am not going to ask you about her father, but if you ever want to talk, I am here for you. I know I am a lot older than you, Sara, but I feel like we could make a life together. I am a man, and you are a beautiful woman. It gets to me sometimes, being in the same house with you. I would never get out of line, and you are safe here, but I would marry you and give you and Molly a home if you would have me. It would make my children happy to have a family again. I would love Molly, and she would not have to know that I wasn't her father. I know this is a lot to put on you. You think about it, and we will talk again soon."

Sara reached over, took Richard's hand, and held it for a minute. "You are the kindest man I have ever known," she said. She looked into his blue eyes, and for the first time, she felt like he could make everything okay. Mr. Preston got up, said good night, and went in the house.

Sara's heart was beating fast, and she felt dizzy. *He wants to marry me and be a father to Molly!* she thought. *He would be a wonderful father, and he could take care of us.* Sara hadn't thought of Warren in a long time, but she did that night. Here was a wonderful man who had not known her and Molly for more than a few months. *He wants to marry me and give me and Molly a home. It sure sounds like it would be a good life. Mr. Preston knows very little about me. I will have to tell him I am only eighteen. And I will have to tell him about Warren.* Sara had told Warren to stay out of her life, so maybe if she married Mr. Preston, he would not be able to find her. She was afraid that some of Warren's family might try to get Molly.

As she went to sleep that night, she prayed that God would help her make the right decision. The next morning, Sara helped the children get off to school, and then she was busy getting the wash hung on the line. There was a nice breeze blowing, and the clothes would smell so fresh when they dried. As she turned around, she saw Patricia coming around the house.

"Hi, Sara, I am so glad to see you!"

"I am glad to see you, Patricia. How are things going down at Miss Davis's?"

"Just the same. I want you to know that Evelyn and Warren came by Miss Davis's home yesterday looking for you. Miss Davis said she didn't know where you had gone. Warren was asking about the baby. Evelyn wanted to know where you were working. I didn't let them see me. Miss Davis said she didn't tell them a thing, but she saw Francis from the cafeteria this morning, and they had been down there asking questions. They probably know you are up here working for Mr. Preston. Why are they asking questions?"

"Warren didn't want us, and Evelyn said the baby wasn't Warren's. You can look at Molly and tell she belongs to Warren. Maybe that is what they want to do. Well, they are not going to get the chance to cause me trouble. I told Warren to stay out of my life, and I meant it. He hurt me, and he's not going to do it again. Come on, Patricia, let's go in the house. It is time for Molly to get up from her nap, and I will fix us a cup of coffee."

They walked in the kitchen. "This is a really nice kitchen," Patricia said. Sara went and got Molly. She was awake and just smiling, such a happy baby.

They had their coffee and decided to go out on the front porch. "The front porch is my favorite place," Sara said. "Molly loves for us to swing." Just as they were getting ready to sit in the swing, Sara looked up to see Warren and Evelyn coming up the walk. "Oh, dear God, don't let this be happening," she breathed.

Patricia looked at Sara and said, "Be calm. You can handle this."

Sara held Molly close to her and said, "What are you two doing here?"

Evelyn spoke up and said, "I want Warren to see this baby so he can get on with his life—so he can stop feeling so guilty."

"You two are not welcome here."

Warren said, "Please, Sara. I just wanted to make sure you were all right."

"It is a little late, Warren. I have a good job and a place to live."

"I want to see your baby."

"She is my baby." Sara's heart was about to explode. She had loved Warren so much, and he had hurt her so badly. "I will let you see her, but then you have to leave and promise me you will never come back into my life again."

Sara turned Molly around, and Warren looked at his baby for the first time and for the last time.

Warren stood there with a look on his face that Sara would never forget. He didn't say anything for a few minutes. Then he said, "She is beautiful, and she looks like me. I am so sorry, Sara." He touched Molly's dark, wavy hair and said, "You take good care of her."

Then Evelyn said, "Okay, so she looks like you. Now she will want money."

Sara spoke up and said, "I want nothing from either of you. Get out of my life, and never ever try to see us again." She knew that Evelyn would never let Warren have any kind of life. Sara did not understand why Warren let her tell him what to do. He was such a weak man to let her run his life. Evelyn hadn't done such a great job on her own life. Her marriage was on the rocks, and she was such a controlling person. It was always her way.

As Warren and Evelyn started to walk away, Sara's eyes met Warren's and she could see that he still loved her. He said, "I'm sorry, Sara, really sorry."

Sara felt like she would die is she had to go through this again. But holding so tight to Molly, she turned and walked away, thinking, *I never want to see them again.* She walked over to Patricia. "He is dead as far as I am concerned. I am putting him out of my life forever. I am going to make a new life for myself and my baby. I didn't know that love could hurt you so bad or that someone could be so mean."

Sara and Patricia went back into the house. Sara said, "I know what I am going to do now!"

"What are you talking about?"

"Mr. Preston asked me if I would marry him."

"He did what?!"

"He said that he would take good care of us, and we could be a family. He is a wonderful man and works hard. His children have been through a lot, and so has he. I really like him, and I know we would have a good life together."

Sara walked out into the back yard to get the sheets off the line. Patricia followed her. "Do you know what you are saying?"

"Yes, I do. Richard will take good care of us, and I will be a good wife to him. He is a lot older in years, but he seems young and smart to me. We will grow to love each other. My mind is made up, and I am going to marry Mr. Preston!"

Chapter

Eleven

It was a cool fall morning. The leaves were falling fast, the beautiful colors blowing through the air. "It won't be long and our porch time will be over. It will get too cold to sit out here." Sara looked over at Richard. "I can't believe we will be married in few days. You know, people are talking about us, and they say it won't last six weeks."

"People are so quick to pop off about other people's business. It will last, I promise you, Sara. We will have a long life together."

Sara had sent word to her sister that she was getting married. The phone rang one afternoon, and she heard a voice say, "Is Sara there?"

Sara said, "Blanche, is that you?"

"It is me."

"Where are you, Blanche? I have missed you so much."

"I have missed you, too. What is this about you getting married?"

"I am marrying a wonderful man, and he is going take care of me and Molly."

"Does he know about—"

"Don't say anything else, Blanche. I don't want to talk about it."

"I will be in town tomorrow. I am coming to Ludlow. I heard there were a lot of jobs available there."

"We have several factories and a lot of restaurants. Please come to the house and see us. I want you to meet Richard and his children."

"Okay, I will be there."

Sara was ironing in the kitchen when she heard someone yell, "Anybody home?" from the front porch. Sara knew that voice. It was her sister Blanche, and she ran to the door. She pushed open the screen door and gave Blanche the biggest hug. "I am so glad you are here!" she exclaimed.

"Me, too! Nice place. Got any coffee?"

"Sure, let's go back to the kitchen."

As Sara was pouring the coffee, Blanche said, "Now, tell me all about the job and the wonderful man who wants to marry you."

"He is a wonderful man, and he is a great father to his three children. He is such a hard worker, and he says he cares about Molly and me."

"Oh, he probably just wants to get you in the sack."

"No, he doesn't, Blanche. He really cares about us!"

"Well, how do you feel about him?"

"I like him a lot. He is kind and nice and very good looking, and he loves Molly."

"So you think that is a good reason to get married?"

"Well, I think we could make a life together because we need each other."

"What about Warren?"

"He is dead, Blanche, as far as I am concerned. I will never let him hurt me again. I think Richard can make me forget him. Anyway, the story I told is that he was killed in a car wreck before Molly was born. I gave Molly his name, and that's the story."

"Will you tell Richard the truth?"

"He has not asked, and he said he didn't care about what happened in the past."

About that time, Donna walked in the room with Molly in her arms. "This is Donna," Sara said.

"Hi, I am Blanche, Sara's sister."

"Nice to meet you," Donna replied.

"She is a pretty baby. Can I hold her?"

"Yes, you can."

"She is a fat one and looks like her mother!"

"Have you heard from Mom and Dad lately?"

"I got a letter from Mom before I left Nashville. Mom said she had not heard from you for a long time."

"Will you write her, Blanche, and tell her about Molly and the story I am telling? They don't need to know anything else. Let her know I am going to marry Mr. Preston."

"When do I get to meet this wonderful man?"

"Do you want to stay for supper?"

"Yes, I do. I also need a place to spend the night."

"I will talk to Richard and see if we can put you up for the night. Why aren't you with Bill?"

"Oh, he lost his job, and I got mad at him for spending what little money we had, so I left him. I told him to get a job, and that I wasn't coming back. I think I might just get a job and stay in this town. It seems like a nice place."

The screen door opened and in ran Larry. "What's for supper?" he asked. "I am hungry." Sara was just taking an apple pie out of the oven. "It smells so good," he said. "Can I have a piece?"

"Not now, Larry, but after supper."

He turned around and saw Blanche. "Who are you?" he asked.

"This is my sister, Larry," Sara answered. "Her name is Blanche."

"Is she going to eat supper, too?"

"Yes, I think so."

"Do you like apple pie?" Larry asked Blanche.

"No, I don't care much for apples."

"That's good," Larry answered, and then he ran off to play with his little toy soldiers.

Blanche helped Donna set the table for supper. Jack had come in and spoken to them, and then Richard came walking into the kitchen. "What's going on in here?" he asked.

"Hi, Richard," Sara said. "This is my sister Blanche. She came into town to see me and Molly."

"Nice to meet you, Blanche. Pull up a chair and have some food. Sara is a good cook."

As they were finishing their food, Richard asked Blanche if she had a place to spend the night.

"No, I don't," she replied.

"We can make you up a bed on the couch if you like."

"That would be nice. Thank you."

The next few days turned into a week, and Blanche had found a job at the Ruby Dot Restaurant a few blocks away. She also had found a sleeping room.

It was a quiet night, and Sara was sewing some buttons on a shirt for Jack. The rain was hitting against the windows when Sara looked up and saw Richard standing there looking at her.

"I can't keep my eyes off of you," he said. "I have fallen in love with you, Sara. I want you for my wife." Richard walked over and pulled her out of the chair. He put his arms around her, put his lips on her lips, and kissed her like she had never been kissed before. When she pulled back a little, he stopped. "I am sorry," he said.

"Don't be sorry. I like it, but I just don't want it to go too far."

Richard put his hand on Sara's face and touched her soft skin. "I want you to be my wife."

"I want that, too. I will be a good wife."

He stroked her long, brown hair. "I will never hurt you, and I will take care of you and Molly forever."

Sara put her arms around Richard and kissed him long and passionately. It made her feel warm all over and safe and alive. She knew everything would be all right. She was falling in love with this wonderful man.

Chapter

Twelve

The sun was shining brightly on a cold winter day. It was the day Sara and Richard were to get married. They were to be at the church at 2 o'clock. Sara was putting on her two-piece suit. It was such a pretty blue suit. Donna had helped her pick it out.

Donna came in holding Molly. "We are ready to go," she said. "How do I look, Donna?"

"You look pretty! Daddy is waiting in the car. Blanche and Bill have already left. Jack and Larry went with them."

As Sara got in the car, she couldn't help but notice how handsome Richard was in his suit. "You look nice, Richard," she said.

"I'd better because I am getting married!" he said.

As they pulled up to the church, everyone was standing outside. The church door was locked. They were supposed to go in the side door. The preacher was waiting there for them.

It was just family who was going to attend the wedding. Bill and Blanche were standing up with them. After they went inside, the preacher asked if everyone was there.

"Yes," Sara said.

"Let's get started."

Richard had a corsage for Sara, and she pinned it on. The preacher said his words and then asked if they had the rings. Sara was so nervous that she could hardly stand still. Richard put the ring on Sara's finger, and she felt so wonderful, and then she put the ring on Richard's hand. Then the preacher said, "I pronounce you man and wife."

Sara said, "I am so happy!"

Richard walked over, picked up Molly, and said, "Now you are my little girl, too!"

Donna said, "I have a little sister."

It was such a happy time. Larry said he really wanted a brother, but he liked Molly so a little sister was okay.

Sara said, "Let's go back to the house and have some wedding cake and punch."

Blanche had gotten them a wedding cake and made the punch so they could have a little reception. Some of Richard's family had stopped by to wish them well. It was a nice day.

Sara was a little nervous about sleeping in Richard's room. There were a lot of people in the house that night. Blanche and Bill were staying the night.

"That's all right," said Richard. "We won't be here. We are going to the hotel. It is our honeymoon night."

"What about Molly?" Sara asked. "She has never been away from me."

"Donna and Blanche will take good care of her. We need a little time to ourselves."

Sara was so excited and happy to be alone with her new husband. She slipped out of her wedding suit and was standing there in her slip brushing her hair. When Richard came into the room, he took Sara's hand and walked her over to the bed. He sat down on the bed and pulled her onto his lap. He gently kissed her neck and said, "I love you, Sara."

When Sara woke up the next morning, she felt like she was dreaming. The sun was shining through the window. She looked over at her new husband who was sleeping. What a wonderful night they had had. Richard was so loving and gentle. It made her think back to Warren and how she had loved him and he hurt her so badly. She knew she could learn to love Richard and that he would never hurt her. Sara had never felt so safe and happy.

The long winter was coming to an end. Spring was just around the corner. Sara was so happy with her new life. Richard was a wonderful husband. Molly was growing like a weed. The older children seemed so happy. Larry was a busy little guy. Sara would sit on the floor and play with his army soldiers with him. Molly would always mess up his army men but he didn't seem to care. Larry always wanted Sara to read to him, but she was always too busy.

One day Sara was in the kitchen making pancakes. Richard had been away at work for a few hours. He would get up extra early and go down to the basement and fire up the coal furnace, so that when the kids got up, it was nice and warm.

Larry came running into the kitchen. "I smell pancakes and I want six!" he cried.

"You must be hungry this morning."

"I am!"

Donna came in carrying Molly. "I think we are all ready for breakfast." Molly was clapping her little hands. They were all sitting down to eat.

"Where is Jack?" Sara asked.

"He was just getting up. He is lazy this morning. He didn't get up and go to work with Daddy this morning. I heard Daddy say he would talk to him this evening. He is in trouble."

Jack pulled his chair up to the table and said, "I am starving for pancakes."

"They sure taste good," said Larry.

The phone rang. Who would be calling so early? Sara got up to answer it. The kids were busy enjoying their pancakes.

Sara said "hello," but there was no answer. She started to hang up, but then a voice said, "How are you, Sara?"

"I am fine." Sara felt like she was going to faint.

"I need to see you and Molly," the voice said.

"I am sorry. You must have the wrong number," Sara said and then she hung up the phone.

Her worst nightmare had come true. It was Warren. What was he doing calling her?

Jack said, "Who was that?"

"Oh, it was the wrong number." Sara's heart was beating so fast that she was afraid the children could see it beating. She felt sick. All she needed was for Warren to show up and cause trouble. He was supposed to be dead. He must be in town. There was no operator on the phone—just him. As Sara hung up the phone, she just felt sick. *What if he keeps calling?* she worried. *He was supposed to stay out of my life. He didn't want us, and now we have a wonderful life.*

Richard had never asked about Warren and how things had happened. Tears started running down Sara's cheeks. She didn't want the children to see her crying. She knew she had to tell Richard the whole story—and she had something else to tell Richard, too.

Chapter

Thirteen

There were signs of spring everywhere. Sara loved to see the trees and flowers growing and the beautiful colors. It would not be long before they could put the porch swing up. Sara was standing at the kitchen sink when Richard walked up behind her and said, "How about some lunch?"

Sara turned around and said, "What are you doing here this time of day?"

"I had to come back into the dairy for another load of milk, and I missed you so much that I had to slip up here to see you." He gave her a loving kiss. "I love you, Sara."

"I have something to tell you, Richard."

"What is it?"

"I am going to have a baby."

"What?!" Richard grabbed Sara and held onto her. "I am so happy! When will the baby come?"

"It will be a few months yet. I have an appointment with the doctor next week."

"Are you feeling okay? Donna said she saw you upset the other day. Is everything all right?"

"Yes, but we do need to talk soon."

"I'd better get back to work. I will see you tonight."

Time was going by so fast. Spring was heading into summer. Molly was walking, and it would not be too long until the new baby arrived.

Sara and Richard were sitting on the front porch enjoying each other's company. They loved their porch time. Sara had not gotten any phone calls lately, so that made her feel better. They talked as they watched the cars go down the street. Larry was playing out on the sidewalk, and Donna was entertaining Molly.

Sara noticed that the same car had passed the house twice going slowly. She looked at the two men in the car, and then looked away. *Oh my Lord, it is Warren!* she thought. Sara got so nervous. *Please, dear God, don't let them stop.*

"What is wrong, Sara?" Richard asked.

"I need to tell you something, Richard. I told you that Molly's father was dead and that I had been married."

"Stop, Sara, it is not important. You are my wife now, and Molly is my little girl. I want to adopt Molly so she will be mine."

"I want her to be yours, but first you must know the truth. Molly's father is not dead."

Richard didn't say anything for a few minutes.

Sara began to explain. "He is dead as far as I am concerned. He didn't want her before she was born, so I am sure he doesn't want her now."

"All I care about, Sara, is you, Molly, my children, and the new baby. We are a family. The past is over, and we have a long wonderful future ahead of us. After the new baby is born, we will go see a lawyer about adopting Molly."

Sara woke Richard up while it was still dark outside. "What is the matter?" he asked.

"I need to go to the hospital. It is time for the baby. I have been having some hard labor pain for a few hours."

Richard jumped up and got into his clothes. Sara put her housecoat on, and they woke up Donna and Blanche to let them know what was going on. Blanche had left Bill again so she was back at Sara's. They just couldn't seem to make their marriage work. Blanche was always so much help for Sara. The Preston house always had room for someone else.

It didn't take long for Sara to have the baby. She was a beautiful blue-eyed blonde-haired girl. She looked just like Richard. The nurse brought her to the window of the nursery. Richard stood there with tears in his eyes. Sara had given him a wonderful baby girl.

He couldn't wait to see Sara. "She will be a little drowsy," the nurse said. "She's had some medicine."

Richard walked up to the bed. Sara's eyes opened. Richard bent down and gave Sara a kiss that said thank you. "She is beautiful, and she looks like me. I am so happy. Molly has a playmate. I hope Larry won't be too disappointed. He wanted a brother."

"He will be just fine. What do you want to name her, Richard?"

"I think Lilly would be nice."

"Then Lilly it is!"

"You get some sleep. You need your rest. I will go home and tell everyone the details." As Richard walked toward the door, he turned around to say goodbye.

Sara said, "I love you, Richard."

"What a wonderful day!" he said as he left the hospital room.

A few days passed, and it was time for Sara and Lilly to come home from the hospital. Everything had gone well while Sara was away. Donna and Blanche had kept things going. Donna was in business college during the day. Blanche was glad she could help out since she was staying there for nothing. It made her feel better to be able to help out.

Larry was still mad about Lilly being a girl. He had even tried to call the hospital to see if he could exchange her for a boy. "I don't want any more girls!" he said. Jack just laughed.

When Molly saw her mother come in the door, she was so happy to see her. She looked at the baby and said, "Baby!" and then went on playing with her toys.

Larry looked at Lilly for a few minutes and then said, "I guess she can stay."

Chapter

Fourteen

Time was passing fast. Sara was back on her feet in no time. Blanche was still with them, and she was so much help. The hospital had sent some papers home with Sara. She was looking at them when Richard came into the kitchen.

"What are you reading, Sara?"

"Oh, just some papers the hospital sent home."

As Richard looked closer, he noticed that the papers were upside down.

"Let me have those papers." Richard had noticed several times before that Sara would avoid reading. "Let me look at those papers."

Sara seemed a little nervous. "Richard, I need to tell you something. I have wanted to tell you before now, but I was afraid you would think badly of me." Sara started to cry. "I can't read or write very well. I am so sorry I didn't tell you before. I can't read much at all. I want to learn, but it seems so hard."

"Don't cry—it will be okay," Richard said. "How do you do everything you do without reading?"

"I have a good memory. Please don't tell anyone. They will think I am stupid."

"I wouldn't tell anyone. That will be our secret, and don't you ever think you are stupid! You a very smart young woman." Richard held Sara in his arms. "I will always take care of you, Sara, and our family. You have given me a beautiful baby girl. I am so happy. I guess I know now why Blanche is so protective of you. She didn't want anyone to know you can't read. She is a lot of help to you with Molly and Lilly. That husband of hers is no good. Blanche is welcome here, but Bill isn't. He is lazy, and I won't have him eating off of us. I work too hard. I will help anyone who will help themselves, but he is just plain lazy."

Life was going well for Sara and Richard. Donna had finished business college and gotten a good job. Jack had decided to go into the air force. Larry had adjusted so well. He loved Sara. He didn't cry at night anymore for his mother. His memory was not as strong as it was for her. And he really liked his little sisters. The house was always full of people. Richard's cousin's wife had passed away and left him with two children. He wasn't a very good father, and he didn't know how to raise children, so most of the time, Eddie, his little son, would be at Richard and Sara's house. Eddie and Larry could get into so much trouble, but Sara would keep them in line.

Chapter

Fifteen

Sara was sitting at her sewing machine. Richard had bought her a Singer. She didn't know how to sew, but she had watched one of her neighbors sew one afternoon, and she told Richard that she could teach herself. Sara could not read a pattern, but she would take a dress and put it on a piece of newspaper and cut out around it. Then she would get material and sew from her own pattern. She was determined to sew, and she learned to make a lot of things. Richard was amazed at what Sara could do.

Sara was swinging on the front porch and Richard was smoking his pipe while Molly and Lilly were playing. The mail had just come, and there was a letter from Jack. "He really likes the air force," Richard read, "and he said to tell you hi, Sara, and that he misses your cooking."

Molly really missed Jack. He would carry her around, and he had spoiled her.

As Sara was swinging, Richard looked over at her and said, "You look so pretty today and so happy. I don't know how you keep everything going so well around here. You are such a good wife, Sara." Richard walked over to the swing, sat down, put his arm around her, and gave her a kiss as he patted her on the leg.

Sara chuckled out loud.

"What's so funny?" Richard asked.

"I was just thinking that every time you kiss me I get pregnant."

Richard looked at Sara and asked, "Are you going to have another baby?"

"Yep. You said you loved babies."

"Oh, Sara, I am so happy! We are sure filling up this house. Have you said anything to Donna?"

"No, you are the first to hear."

The months passed fast, and another beautiful baby girl had become the newest member of the Preston house. Her name was Lucy. She had light brown hair and brown eyes. "She looks like both of us," Sara told Richard.

Larry told Sara he wished that hospital would stop sending little baby girls home. He would like a boy! The Preston house was a busy place and a happy home. Sara could not be any happier. Time was going by fast. Blanche had come back to stay for awhile. She and Bill had gotten divorced. He didn't want to work, and she didn't want to settle down. She had a bit of a wild streak in her. Sara was glad to have her back. She was a lot of help with the children. Sara loved Blanche so much, and they were very close.

Blanche would always read for Sara. Sara was still so afraid that someone might find out that she couldn't read. She was so smart in so many things. She could even write a few names, the ones she had to know.

One day Sara and Blanche took the girls to the park. They had packed a lunch, and it was a beautiful day. The girls loved to play at the park, and it was only a few blocks from the house, so it was always a nice walk.

Sara and Blanche sat watching the girls play, when Sara said, "I am so lucky to have married Richard. He is so good to me, and I have grown to love him so much. He is such a wonderful father to all the children. He just loves babies, and the girls are not babies anymore."

"Well, it's probably time for another," Blanche joked.

Sara looked at Blanche and just smiled.

"You're not pregnant again?"

"Yep, I am."

"Oh, my goodness! You are a baby factory! Have you told Richard?"

"I am going to tell him tonight. I know he will be happy."

Chapter

Sixteen

The seasons had changed again, and fall was in the air. The new baby had arrived, and she was a dark-haired blue-eyed girl they named Annie. She was beautiful. Sara and Richard were the talk of the neighborhood. The marriage they hadn't thought would last six weeks had already lasted almost six years and was still going strong. They had made a wonderful, big family. Richard worked hard to provide for all their needs. There always seemed to be someone else who needed help, and there was always room for one more at the supper table. Sara could stretch a meal to feed more, and she did so many times. Sara's sister and family from up north would always drop in on their way south for a free meal and a place to sleep. Richard was always helping out his brother when he was out of work. It took everything that he made to provide for his own family, but he was so good at managing his money and helping out people who needed help.

Sara was watching the children play when Richard walked up the back sidewalk. He had been out in the shed, and he had a serious look on his face.

"What is wrong, Richard?" Sara asked.

"Well, I have been thinking that it is time that I adopt Molly and give her my name."

"Molly will never know any difference. It is just a lot of paper work."

"You said that her father was dead so there should not be any problems."

Sara said, "All right."

"I will see the lawyer tomorrow."

Sara wanted Richard to adopt Molly, but she was so afraid that her lies would cause problems. But Warren hadn't wanted her, so why would he even care if she was adopted? Sara worried all night and the next day.

Richard came in from work. He had a hard day, but he had good news. Mr. Harris, the lawyer, said that all they had to do was bring her birth certificate, fill out the papers, and then she would be his. Richard was so happy.

"That is all we have to do?" Sara asked.

"Well, we have to run a notice in the paper in the town that Warren is from, stating that she is being adopted. So, if anyone has a problem with it, they can notify the lawyer. They give them about ten days to do so."

Sara felt sick. *What if they try to cause trouble?* she wondered. *What will I do?*

Richard could see the panic in her eyes. "Don't worry, Sara. They don't want Molly," he reassured her. "They have never tried to do one thing for her. I have taken care of her, and she is going to be mine. I love her like she is mine."

Sara had not told Richard that Warren's mother had called her a few times trying to ask about Molly. Sara would not talk to her. Sara could not tell Richard the truth—that Warren was really alive. He would think she was terrible, and maybe he would not want her anymore. Sara was upset all week while waiting to hear from the lawyer. She was so afraid that Warren's family would try to cause trouble—not because they wanted Molly, but just because she thought they were mean like Evelyn.

Richard told Sara not to worry, that everything would be all right. Richard was a smart man, and he never asked Sara any questions about Warren being dead. He knew she thought she had to protect herself, but also he knew she was young and had to tell her story. He loved Sara and Molly, and he didn't care about her past. Richard was only concerned about their future. The days had passed, and Sara had heard nothing from Warren's family about the notice in the paper for Molly's adoption.

The time had come to go to the lawyer's office to sign the papers. Richard told Sara that this was a wonderful day! He would be Molly's father, and she would not have to ever know who her real father was. Sara knew that Richard would always love her just the same way he loved all of his other children.

Chapter

Seventeen

The years flew by. Jack got married to a nice girl. Donna got married to a great guy. Larry and the little girls just loved their new family members. Donna was so great. She was always taking Molly, Lilly, Lucy, and Annie to great places, like ice skating, to the movies, and to the library. The girls just loved all the special things. Sara was so grateful for all that Donna did for her.

Donna was so good to help the girls with their homework. Donna had suspected that Sara could not read, but she never said anything—she just would step in and help. Richard would always help the girls. He was so busy. He would work all day on the milk route and then a couple nights a week. He had to do his bills for customers. Sara knew she was so blessed. He was a wonderful husband and father. The children loved their daddy so much. Sara would have them all cleaned up for Richard when he came home from work. They always ran to meet him at the door to see who could get the first kiss.

Larry had gotten his driver's license and was always trying to get the car keys. Richard would let him use the car on special occasions.

Sara and Richard were sitting on the front porch talking and holding hands. Their love had grown deeper than either one of them had ever dreamed it would. But it was so hard to get time alone with such a full house. This was one of those times when they had a few minutes alone together. Sara looked in Richard's eyes and said, "You have been the best husband and father. I am so happy, and I love you so much."

Richard pulled Sara close and kissed her passionately. "I love you, too, Sara. You have made my life complete." Sara loved for Richard to kiss her. He was so loving, and he always told her how pretty she was. He made her feel wonderful.

As Sara and Richard sat on the porch, he reached over, picked up her hand, and kissed it. The rain had started to come down. "I love the smell of rain and the sound it makes," said Richard. "Always remember that I love you more than all the rain drops."

Sara had just reached up to kiss him when Molly, Lilly, Lucy, and Annie all came running out on the porch. All of them were trying to get up on Daddy's lap to get some kisses of their own.

Sara got up and let the girls have their time. "I am going to go in and pop some corn for all of us," she said. Richard and the girls loved their popcorn.

It was a nice summer evening. The girls were playing with the neighbor children, and Sara was making cherry jelly. The cherry tree had put out a good crop this year. Sara had to pick them fast because the children could clean that tree. They ate them as soon as they started turning red.

Molly came into the kitchen where Sara was cleaning up. She was crying. "What's wrong, Molly?" Sara asked. "Are you hurt?"

"No, I am not hurt." But she couldn't stop crying.

"Tell me what is wrong!"

"They said Daddy wasn't my Daddy." She started crying harder.

"Who said that?"

"Joyce next door said I didn't belong to him. What does that mean?"

Sara started getting upset herself. "Joyce doesn't know what she is talking about. She is just being a mean girl. You are your Daddy's little girl." Sara had never planned on telling Molly the truth. Now what was she going to do?

Sara tried to calm Molly down. "It is all right, Molly. Don't' cry."

Molly finally stopped crying and looked up at Sara. "So, Joyce was just being mean?"

"Yes, she was, but I do have to tell you something. Your daddy and I were not ever going to tell you that he is not your real father."

Molly started to cry again. It was hard for her to understand this at ten years old. Sara said, "Stop crying and listen to me. Your real father was killed in a car wreck before you were born, and when you were just a few weeks old, I met Richard and we got married. The first time Richard saw you he fell in love with you. He picked you out to be his little girl. So, you are special, and he loves you just the same as all the other children."

Molly got real quiet for a few minutes. Then Sara said, "We will not talk about this anymore. We are all one family. I don't want anyone to know about this. When you get older, if you want to know anything about your real father, I will tell you what I know."

Sara told Richard what happened, and he was upset that Molly had to be told.

"I don't think she really understands, and she didn't want to talk about it, and neither do I," Sara said.

"Molly is mine, just like the rest of the children," Richard affirmed.

The weeks passed, and nothing else was said. Sara did tell Joyce's mother what she had done, and of course, Joyce said she hadn't said anything. But Sara knew that Joyce probably heard her parents talking about her and Richard. Neighbors loved to gossip.

Chapter

Eighteen

Sara and Richard were very happy. Richard worked hard to provide for Sara and the children. They were all in grade school now. Larry was getting ready to go to a junior college in Oklahoma. His cousin lived out there and was going to school there. Sara and Richard had saved and cleaned houses for some people to make some extra money to send Larry to college. Larry promised to study hard, even though he had to work and make his own spending money. The day that Larry left for college he told Sara thanks for all she had done for him. He had never called her "Mother"—only "Sara." He could remember his own mother some, but he was grateful that she had been there in his life.

Molly, Lilly, Lucy, and Annie would miss Larry. He was always doing things to make them laugh and to get them in trouble. Larry said he would write often, and Sara felt a little sad because she knew she would never be able to read Larry's letters. Sara still kept her secret hidden.

A few months had passed, and things were going well. The girls were still taking turns sleeping in Larry's room. He had had a small bedroom off the kitchen. It had once been a back porch, but as the Preston family grew, the house had to grow, too. Sara was always doing something in the house, knocking out walls and putting up new ones. She was a great one for remodeling the house. She could start it, and then Richard would have to hire someone to finish the project! Richard came home from work one day and found Sara covered in dirt. She had decided they needed a basement under the house and so she had started digging. Richard could not believe his eyes. Sara was covered in dirt, and all you could see were the whites of her big brown eyes. Richard started to get mad, but then he got so tickled, he started laughing. Sara had Molly, Lilly, Lucy, and Annie carrying buckets of dirt out in the back yard. The children were having so much fun in the dirt. Richard walked over to Sara, took the shovel out of her hand, and gave her a kiss on her lips. "What have you gotten us into now?" he asked. She started telling Richard about her plan for the basement. There was never a dull moment in their house.

Sara was busy working in the kitchen. It would soon be Christmas, and Larry would be home for the holidays. He was doing well in college. There was a light dusting of snow on the ground. The children were trying to get enough together to make a snowman; it wasn't working, but they were having fun.

Sara put some milk on the stove to make hot cocoa. She knew the girls would be in soon. The phone rang, and so Sara turned off the milk as she headed for the phone. She said hello, but no one answered.

"Hello?" said a voice. "I want to talk to Sara."

"This is Sara. Who is this?"

"I am Warren's mother."

Sara didn't say a word—she just froze.

"Don't hang up, Sara," the voice said. "I want to talk to you."

"We don't have anything to talk about. I told Warren and Evelyn to stay out of my life, and I meant it."

"I just wanted to know how Molly was."

"Molly is fine. She knows nothing about you people, and that the way it is going to stay. Warren wanted nothing to do with us. Richard adopted Molly, and she is his now."

"Oh, yes, we saw the notice in the paper."

"So you know she has a good life. Why do you care now when you didn't before?"

"I didn't know everything that happened. Molly is my grandchild."

"No, she is not. Do not call here again. You will cause trouble. You hurt us once, now leave us alone." When Sara hung up the phone, she was shaking all over.

The girls came running into the kitchen, wet from head to toe. "Take off those wet clothes and lay them on the register!" Sara said. The heat from the coal furnace put out a lot of nice, warm heat.

Sara poured everyone a cup of hot cocoa. Her hands were shaking as she poured the last cup. She was so upset over that phone call. *If only they would just leave me alone. What if Molly had answered the phone?*

Mrs. Evans had told her who she was and that made Sara sick to think about that. She had never told Richard about the phone calls from Mrs. Evans. She prayed she would never call there again.

The holidays came, and Larry was home. It was a wonderful time. The house was full of family, and the big tree at the front window was surrounded by lots of presents. Richard always had his big bowl of fruit and nuts. He would crack the nuts and give each of the girls a piece. Sara told Richard, "If you were eating dirt, those girls would want some, too."

Sara kept busy in the kitchen. The smells from her baking filled the house. It was a wonderful Christmas. She was so happy—her life had become more than she ever dreamed it would be. She loved Richard very much, and she had been able to keep her past hidden. Her only fear was that some of Warren's family would try to cause her trouble or get to Molly and tell her that she hadn't been married to Warren. Every once in a while she thought she saw Warren in a crowd of people. She would dream that Warren would come take Molly away. Sara would sometimes wake up screaming from this nightmare. But Richard would always make everything okay. She knew he would take care of everything. Sara always referred to Warren as being dead, but Richard knew that he was probably alive even though he never said anything about it. Sara had her own story about what happened, and he just let her have it.

Chapter

Nineteen

The years passed, and the girls were becoming teenagers. Molly and Lilly were very close; they ran around together and had a lot of the same friends. Lucy and Annie played together a lot. They were close in age, and everyone always said what nice and pretty girls they were.

The Preston's house was always full of friends. Sara always let the girls have their friends spend the night. Sara and Richard were on the front porch when the girls came home, and they each had a friend. They all had their overnight bags—they were having a slumber party. Sara looked at Richard and smiled. "At least we know where they are," she said.

"Yes, we do, but you know the boys will be hanging around later. I will run them off when it gets late."

It didn't take long, and the boys were there to see the girls. Sara said, "You can talk on the porch for a while if you don't get too loud."

Molly had her eye on one boy, and Lilly liked one of the boys, too. Gary was a couple of years older than Molly. He would tell her, "When you grow up, we will go out." Gary was cute, and Molly loved to flirt with him. He had just gotten his driver's license. But Molly knew she could not go out in a car with boy until she was fifteen.

The Preston's house was a busy and fun place, with four teenagers living there. There was never a dull moment.

Sara was always busy sewing for the girls. She could make anything. All she had to do was study the pattern and she could cut it out and sew it up. Richard worked hard for his family. One of the girls was always needing shoes.

One Sunday afternoon, Sara and Richard sent the girls to the movies. It was so hard for them to have any time alone. As Richard took Sara into his arms and kissed her, she said, "Thank you, honey."

As Richard looked into Sara's eyes, he said, "You have made my life complete."

"I don't know what would have happened to Molly and me if you had not come into our lives. You are a wonderful husband, but you also have taught me so much about life and helped me with my reading."

Sara continued, "Richard, I am so ashamed that I can't read or write much. I think I would just die if anyone knew. They would think I was stupid."

"You are not stupid, Sara. You are very smart. Just look at what you have done in your life! You didn't get the opportunity to go to school very much, but you could fool the Queen of England. You can talk to anyone, and they would never know that you couldn't read. I told you I would take care of you, and when I am gone, Donna and Jack will help you whenever you need help. We are a strong family. I think that you are the strongest and bravest person I have ever known. I am so proud that you are the mother of my children."

As they held each other in their arms, Sara knew that she could never love another man the way she loved Richard. He had shown her what real love was.

Chapter

***

Twenty

Spring had come again, and life was normal at the Preston's house. The girls were looking forward to summer break. Molly was still seeing Gary. Sara and Richard liked him, but Richard said that Molly was too young to get too serious. The other girls were just dating and having fun. Molly was in a hurry to grow up.

Sara was ironing when Molly came in the kitchen. Molly sat down at the table and said, "I need to ask you something."

"What do you want to ask?"

There was a long pause, and then Molly said, "What did he look like?"

Sara knew at once who she was talking about, and so she began to describe Warren for her daughter. "He was very handsome. He had dark black brown, wavy hair and blue eyes. Sometimes they looked blue and green. He was short."

"What was his name?"

"His name was Warren. We were married, and he was killed in a car wreck before you were born."

Sara had told the story so often she almost believed it herself.

"Do I look like him?" Molly asked.

"Yes, you do."

"Do you have a picture of him?"

"No, I don't have anything of his except a silver ring he gave me." Sara walked over to her purse and pulled out the tarnished little ring. "Here, you can have it."

Molly took the ring and held it in her hand. "Was this your wedding band?"

Sara didn't say anything for a minute. Then she said, "Yes, it was." Sara felt sad and sick at the same time. She didn't want Molly to ask any more questions. She wanted to forget about the past, and she didn't want Molly to know anything about it—maybe someday but not now. Sara's greatest fear was that someone from Warren's family would get to Molly and tell her about Sara and Warren. If Evelyn ever told her side, it would be terrible. Sara had never told anyone the whole truth—not even Richard. She never would say that Warren was alive. Sara wanted her story to be true. She almost believed it herself. Richard knew that Warren was probably alive, but he never let Sara know that he thought that.

Sara felt sad that she couldn't tell Molly the real story, but she was so ashamed of what had happened. Sara didn't want anyone to think she wasn't a good person.

Sara and Richard had gone for a walk over to the park. There was a baseball game going on, and Richard loved to watch the kids play ball. Sara asked him if he thought Molly was acting differently.

"No, I think she acts the same, except she is too crazy over that Gary," Richard replied. "I wish she didn't see him so much. He is a good boy, but they are all after the same thing at his age. I told Molly and Lilly they have to watch the boys. I know they are good girls, but good girls can get in trouble. I think Molly is just lovesick over Gary."

Sara told Richard that Molly had asked about Warren.

"Why would she want to know about him?" he asked. "He never did anything for her. I am her father, and I am the one who has raised her."

"I know, and she knows that, too, but I guess she is just curious." Sara could see that it really upset Richard that Molly was interested in Warren, and so she changed the subject. She sat quietly as they finished watching the game.

A few days passed, and everything was going well. Sara was busy working on one of her sewing projects when Molly and Lilly came into the living room. "What are you girls up to?" Sara asked.

"Could we go to the drive-in tonight with Gary?" Molly asked.

Lilly said, "There is a great movie showing, so can we go?"

"Only if you take Lucy and Annie."

"What?!"

"It won't hurt to take them," Molly said. So they popped a bag of popcorn, and off they went. Molly would do anything to get to spend time with Gary. Molly had fallen in love with him, and she wanted to get married. Sara was all for it. She knew that if Molly got married, her name would change, and then Warren's family could never find her. After all, where she came from, the girls got married early in life. But Richard said that Molly could not get married until she graduated from high school. Gary had graduated last year, and he was joining the air force. He knew that that way he would be able to support them both. All Molly could think about was finishing school so she could get married.

Sara couldn't help but think about Molly and Gary getting married and moving away. Sara knew that she would miss Molly, but she wanted to get her away from the phone calls. Warren's mother had called again, wanting to know all about Molly. Sara could not talk to her. Every time she would call, it would cause Sara to have nightmares. She would wake up in the middle of the night screaming, but she would never tell Richard what the dreams were about. Sara sometimes felt like her heart was going to beat out of her chest. She kept so many things to herself. She had to work so hard to keep people from finding out that she couldn't read. Richard would always tell her not to worry. He would take care of everything—and he did.

Chapter

Twenty-One

$\mathbb{R}$ichard was at work when a man approached him and asked, "Are you Mr. Preston?"

"Why, yes, I am."

"I have a letter for you."

"Who are you?"

"I am no one you know," the man said. "I was just asked to give this to you."

Richard took the letter, and the man walked away. Richard finished checking out at the dairy, and as he walked to the car, he remembered the letter. As he got in the car, he opened the letter. It read:

"Mr. Preston, You don't know me, but I just wanted to thank you for what you have done for Molly. I don't know Molly, and I will never know her. I am sure you love her enough for both of us. I am sorry for the hurt that I caused Sara, but I know she has a wonderful life with you. I don't expect you to think much of me, but I do hope that you won't hate me. I am not very well, so I wanted to let you know that my loss was your gain, and just maybe someday she might want to know

that I wasn't a bad guy. I know you will keep this just between us. I don't have much to live for. I destroyed the good things in my life, so I am just waiting out my time. Warren."

Richard tore up the letter. He wasn't very impressed. He thought that Warren's guilt was getting to him and he wanted to clear his conscience. Richard knew he would never tell Sara about the letter. He would not ever let her know that Warren was alive. At least he knew Warren would never try and see Molly. Warren gave up that right when he let Richard adopt her. *She is my daughter, and that's the way it will stay,* he thought.

A few months had passed, and Molly was going to be married. Richard had given his permission. Molly had told Richard how much she loved him and what a wonderful dad he was. She had gotten her high-school diploma like he had asked. Molly had saved every penny she could get her hands on. They had set the date. Gary was away in the air force. Sara had helped get things ready for the wedding. Donna helped as much as she could. She was getting ready to have her fifth baby. Jack's wife had taken Molly shopping for a negligee for her honeymoon. Molly was so excited that she could hardly wait for her wedding day. She knew it would be wonderful. Her sisters would be in the wedding. It would be small but nice. Molly told Gary that she wanted to be married to him and that someday she would have her own family. "I want to have two children," she said. They would be hers, and family was so important to her. She hated the fact that she had no full-blooded sister or brother. There had been a hole in her heart ever since she was told that Richard wasn't her real father. It made her sad, but she couldn't imagine loving her daddy or her brothers and sisters any more than what she did.

Sara was standing in the back of the church, and she was so happy for Molly and Gary. Their wedding day had finally arrived. Richard walked over and put his arm around Sara. "I still think she is too young, but Gary will make a good husband, and he is a hard worker," he said.

The church was full, and everyone was waiting for the bride to come down the aisle.

The music started, and Richard walked Molly down the aisle. Gary was standing there waiting for his bride. All Molly could think about was her new life. She was so grown up for a girl her age.

The next morning came so fast. Molly and Gary had gone for a short honeymoon. Sara was putting away some of the wedding gifts. Molly and Gary wouldn't be able to take much with them. They had to go up to Massachusetts where Gary was stationed with the air force.

The time had come for Molly and Gary to leave, and the car was packed. Molly had never been away from home before. She knew she would miss her family, but she was going to have a new life with Gary.

Sara was so happy for Molly and Gary. She knew she would miss Molly, but she just wanted her to be where no one from Warren's family could find her. Richard had driven the milk truck up to the house so he could say goodbye to Molly. Molly had told Donna and her family goodbye last night. She had called Jack, and he had told her to have a safe trip and to stay in touch. Molly was so lucky to have Donna and Jack. They were wonderful to her. Molly hugged and kissed Lilly, Lucy, and Annie. "Please write to me," she said.

"We will," said the girls.

Sara and Richard walked out to the car. Sara could feel the lump in her throat. She knew she could not cry. Sara had loved and protected Molly for so long that she felt like now Molly would be in good hands with Gary. Sara's life before Richard would be safe. Sara wanted to keep her life a secret. There were some things that were better not told. Sara had told Molly she had been adopted by Richard, her real father's name, and that he was killed before she was born.

Molly seemed to be satisfied with that, and Sara just hoped that Molly would just forget about it now that she was married and starting a new life.

Sara and Richard said goodbye to Molly and Gary.

Molly kissed Richard and said, "I love you, Daddy."

Richard just smiled and said, "You are supposed to!"

As they watched the car drive away, Sara held onto Richard's hand, fighting back the tears. Richard held Sara and said, "It will be just fine." Sara thanked Richard for being such a wonderful husband and father. Sara knew in her heart that she was so blessed to have had the life that she had. She told Richard she looked forward to all the wonderful years ahead of them.

As they sat down on the porch swing, Sara looked over at Richard and said, "We have put a lot of miles on this old swing!"

"Yes, we have," Richard agreed as he leaned over and kissed her.

"I love you, Richard," Sara said.

To order additional copies of

Sara's Secret Journey

have your credit card ready and call
1 800-917-BOOK (2665)

or e-mail
orders@selahbooks.com

or order online at
www.selahbooks.com

www.ingramcontent.com/pod-product-compliance
Lightning Source LLC
Chambersburg PA
CBHW031315060726
47590CB00003B/1221